OFFICIAL NEW KIDS ON THE BLOCK™

ON TOUR

Written by

Justine Korman

Winterland
productions
ROCK EXPRESS ®

A GOLDEN BOOK • NEW YORK

Western Publishing Company, Inc., Racine, Wisconsin 53404

Contents

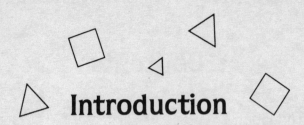

Introduction

Sure you wish you could tour with New Kids on the Block—who doesn't? But if you aren't part of the band family, here's the next best thing.

Grab a suitcase, and don't forget to pack your dreams. This book is your ticket to Tokyo with dashing Danny Wood; to London with jaunty Jonathan Knight; to Hollywood with dreamy Donnie Wahlberg; to New York City with jazzy Jordan Knight; and to Boston with the blue-eyed babe, Joe McIntyre.

Along the way you'll find Tour Trivia questions to test how much you really know about the Fab Five on the road. Look for the answers at the back of this book.

Hurry up, Fab Five fans! This tour is too cool.

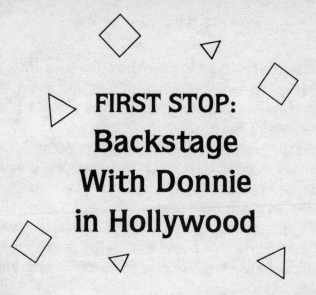

FIRST STOP:
Backstage
With Donnie
in Hollywood

Sometimes Donnie gets this overwhelming feeling of living in his own dream-come-true. Here he is, cruising Hollywood in a limousine, palm trees brushing pink clouds against the dusky blue sky. The New Kids are stuck in a traffic jam, and brake lights are flashing red all down the freeway. But Donnie doesn't mind, because they're headin' toward a screaming-room-only sold-out house—and this is what he's always wanted!

Before he joined the New Kids, Donnie had never even been outside of Boston. Hollywood was just a magical name, a place where people were stars.

But it's real, and it even has real traffic jams. And the New Kids are playing a big show tonight! Donnie's feet tap the limo floor. He wants to be dancing. He wants to be out there in front of the fans!

The conversation between the other guys drifts by Donnie in waves. Right now Jon's talking about the Galleria in nearby Los Angeles, the mall that started it all for valley girls.

Good ol' Jon can't wait to hit the mall and Rodeo Drive, the heart of the Beverly Hills shopping district. Yeah, Beverly Hillbilly Hills is a real place, too, and Donnie Wahlberg from Boston has been there!

Donnie always wanted to be "someone." Maybe everyone dreams of being a star. It seemed pretty farfetched while he was growing up, but Donnie kept hoping and trying.

When he was really little, Donnie wanted to be a baseball star. Then he discovered music.

And, of course, he couldn't wait to have a band! When he was ten, Donnie started one called Risk with his friends Billy and Eric.

The boys didn't know what they were doing! They played everything by ear. Sometimes it worked, and that would be great. Most of the time it didn't work. But Donnie loved it anyway!

He's always been creative. He likes to express himself—in clothes, in music, in rap, or just in words. When he was twelve, Donnie wrote his own comic books and stories. He still likes to draw sometimes. But it isn't the same as performing in front of a live audience—nothing is!

Danny and Donnie got together at the William

Monroe Trotter School in Boston, where they quickly discovered that they both loved music. With a couple of other friends they formed a band called The Kool-Aid Bunch.

Donnie wrote rap routines for the band to perform at parties. When the girls screamed for more, Donnie knew this was what he wanted to do.

Donnie loves being the center of attention, which wasn't easy in a family of nine kids. He was the class clown in school, and he made good grades, too. He just can't resist making people laugh! Around his neighborhood, Donnie was famous for his Michael Jackson imitation—which is what he performed for his New Kids audition.

It's funny that at first Donnie was too scared to try out. He was sure Maurice, their producer, was looking for a really great singer. And Donnie was feeling pretty bad about his singing after Danny got into the school chorus and he didn't.

TOUR TRIVIA

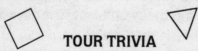

1. Rules in the meet-and-greet room back-stage include:
    a. no autographs
    b. yes, photos
    c. yes, hugging
    d. all of the above

Donnie's friends kept at him. They knew that deep down he really wanted to audition and that he'd regret it if he didn't at least try. Finally, Donnie took the risk... and the rest is history!

Traffic's finally moving again in a steady stream of white and red. Donnie's still used to the street life of Boston, goin' everywhere on sneaker power. But here in California, it's all cars.

Jordan wants a Porsche. Joe is still waiting to get a driver's license. And Donnie's not sure what car he wants—except he knows he wants vanity plates. He loves reading the crazy things people put on them. It's fun! And why not make a statement?

Sometimes Donnie just has to speak out. Some people think he's too outrageous, but Donnie can't change who he is. And if he's a little too much for some people, so be it.

One of the things that really gets Donnie mad is when reporters say New Kids on the Block is only a bubble-gum band that won't last. The guys are serious about their music and their careers. And Donnie thinks New Kids is getting better every day.

All the guys are growing as musicians and learning a lot about the technical side of things, like sound recording and producing. Donnie is serious about The Crickets (the boys' writing/production/engineering team), and about making the Northside Posse the hottest rap group in the country. But most of all, he wants to give the best show in Hollywood tonight!

The limo pulls up to the theater, and girls mob it from all sides, even though it's hours till the performance. Donnie wants to hang out and sign autographs, but Jon says they've got to do the sound check with plenty of time for the crew to fix up the system if anything goes wrong—like what happened one night in New York.

Back then, the New Kids were still lip-synching to prerecorded tracks—it takes money and equipment to set up a live band! Anyway, the sound suddenly went totally dead in the middle of the performance. Show-biz pro Donnie thought, "The show must go on!" So he said, "Sing a cappella." (That means without music.) It worked out pretty well!

Donnie doesn't really have a "type." Superficial things like hair and eye color don't matter to him as much as a girl's personality—and he doesn't care what race, shape, or size she is.

Donnie likes a strong, independent girl who won't rely on him for a personality. And he wants a girl to like him for who he is—not just because he's in a group.

Bisquit, Robo, Tony, and Al, the New Kids' bodyguards, clear a path through the screaming fans. The Fab Five wave to everybody and tell them to come back after the show. It's hard to make them understand that the guys have got to stay focused before a show. There's lots to do.

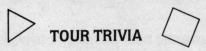 **TOUR TRIVIA**

2. Donnie never travels anywhere without his...

   a. teddy bear
   b. Louis Vuitton bag
   c. tie
   d. tutu

The crew arrived early to set up all the equipment, but it has to be tested and adjusted for levels and feedback long before the audience arrives. The sound check is the New Kids' chance to jam together on their instruments.

Donnie loves the drums, and he's really trying hard to get better. Drumming is sort of like dancing—you feel the beat all through your body. It's way cool!

In the dressing room, there's a pot of tea, honey, and lemon for the guys to drink before the show. Greg McPherson, their music director, says it helps the boys sing better. Donnie would rather have a glass of water, but if tea will make him sing better...down the hatch!

Donnie never shaves before a concert. It's kind of a superstition. He thinks Don Johnson and George Michael are totally chillin'. Besides, it isn't easy shaving when you're all keyed up for a show.

The guys joke around while they pick out outfits for the show. Donnie will wear faded jeans, ripped all across the front of the legs, of course, and a really funky T-shirt he bought in New York. And he doesn't go anywhere without his peace-symbol necklace. It's not just a lucky charm, it's something Donnie believes in.

Donnie likes to wear his baseball hats the wrong way, or high tops with a tuxedo. Sometimes he even wears his jeans inside out. It's just a fun thing to do to shake things up sometimes and be different.

Donnie thinks it's fun to try all kinds of clothes. You never know what you might like! Sometimes he'll experiment with a really conservative jacket, something Jon would wear, and see how it feels. But Donnie won't wear ties. They choke him!

Most people get too embarrassed to do outrageous things. But Donnie says, Who cares? Have fun!

One Halloween he even wore his sister's ballet tutu. His mom still laughs every time she tells the story. What a thrill!

Donnie can't wait to go on. But there's still time before the house will open, then time for the crowd to take its seats, and finally the two opening acts. Donnie heads for the "meet-and-greet" room, where there are plenty of pretty hands to be kissed.

When it's almost time to go on, the Fab Five get in a huddle and yell. Then they start throwing fake punches and shaking one another up to get themselves going. But Donnie's already up!

He hears the audience screaming, "We want the New Kids. We love the New Kids!" And his legs jolt like they want to run onstage without him.

But Donnie waits with the guys while the announcer asks, "Are you ready for showtime?" Donnie's heart starts doing double time. His fingers tingle.

Every show is different. You never know what's going to happen. Each audience is different, and it's time to get onstage and meet this one...NOW!

The guys run past their manager and slap his hand. This is it! As they fly out of the wings, the announcer shouts, "Let's hear it for the New Kids...on the Block!"

Donnie likes a lot of sounds, but there is nothing like applause.

He waits for it to die down a little, then shouts into the mike, "HOLLYWOOOOD, CALIFORNIAAAAA!" And the audience screams back!

He asks, "Are you feelin' good?"

The first few times they answer him, the audience is a little shy. Then they really get screaming, and the guys know it's going to be a great show!

Donnie looks around the audience. He likes to see all the fans and let them know he cares and he's glad they came. Sometimes girls travel a long distance to see a New Kids concert, which means a lot to Donnie!

He likes emceeing almost as much as he likes singing. Donnie makes sure each section of the crowd gets equal attention. It's fun to flirt!

The New Kids do most of their dancing in unison. But each guy also likes to move in his own way sometimes, doin' whatever comes to mind.

Donnie wishes he could spin like Danny, but each guy has his own style. Donnie's into what he calls macho dancing. It's fun to strut across the stage. Danny does bowlegged dances in his baggy shorts, and the fans go crazy. Jordan does the coolest Elvis.

 TOUR TRIVIA

3. While taping the Arsenio Hall Show, the New Kids got to meet...

   a. boxer Mike Tyson
   b. Donnie's favorite actress, Cher
   c. the President
   d. Tiffany

Donnie doesn't notice the set anymore—it's just something the crew has to set up in each new town. But sometimes, out of the corner of his eye, he'll glimpse the cityscape or the rusty scaffolding, and just for a moment, it feels like Boston.

Most of the time, a concert goes by in an intense blur. Donnie concentrates on the music, and his body moves to the beat.

Sometimes he'll suddenly lock eyes with a fan, and for a moment, the whole auditorium drops away and it's just the two of them. Then the music moves on!

Donnie likes to pull one girl onstage and share a moment with her. That's really special.

The New Kids do a mix of slow and funky songs. Donnie likes to sit down and really pour his heart out for the ballads. But it's the fast numbers he gets wild on.

Sometimes the New Kids really cut loose onstage. Once they shot water guns at their opening act, Tommy Page. And during Tommy's final song, "A Zillion Kisses," they threw zillions of chocolate kisses at him. (Tommy got his revenge with Ping-Pong balls during "He'll Be Loving You.") Donnie likes to play onstage.

The New Kids never know how an audience will respond to a new song. They just have to try it out! Donnie feels nervous whenever they first do a new song. But what an incredible charge when you watch an audience hearing something for the first time and liking it!

Donnie's ears ring with screams and applause.

It's over.

The guys say good night to the crowd, and after a lot more screaming, the fans start heading home.

Donnie's always on cloud nine after a show—especially a good one. It's hard to know where to put the leftover energy. He's tired, but he feels too good to sleep.

Backstage, the New Kids sometimes meet celebrities who've come to see the show, like Elton John, Soleil Moon Frye, or Tommy Puett. And, of course, they get to work with famous people like Arsenio Hall when they were on his show.

It still feels strange to Donnie to meet people he looked up to as "stars"—and to realize that somewhere along the line, he became one, too. At least people treat him that way. Inside, he feels the same.

Donnie hopes the New Kids can make something good come out of being stars. The group supports the fight against drug abuse because they've all seen the damage drugs can do.

Donnie urges fans to choose dreams over drugs. He thinks it's important to go for whatever you want and to keep trying whatever your dream is.

As the guys work their way through the fans to the limo, Donnie suddenly realizes he's wiped! Joe yawns.

Danny admires the clay tile roofs on the spotlit mansions they pass on the way to the hotel.

"There's a heavy Spanish influence on architecture all over California," he says, but Donnie's too tired to pay attention.

He's thinking of old friends at home in Boston, and his family. "Uncle Donnie" wonders how much his baby nephew, Adam, has grown.

Donnie pictures his room at home. One wall is a collage he made of pictures of album covers and different things. His mom covered two other walls with pictures from fans.

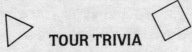

TOUR TRIVIA

4. The New Kids have opened for...
    a. Lisa Lisa
    b. Cult Jam
    c. The Four Tops
    d. all of the above

Along with his bed, dresser, and baseball gear, Donnie's room holds a new drum set and heaps of sentimental stuff. He saves everything!

Donnie has piles of souvenirs and gifts from fans, and tons of junk he can't seem to throw out—like old drawings, toys, and stuffed animals, and the red-leather Michael Jackson jacket he bought with his birthday money when he turned twelve.

Donnie knows he doesn't seem like the sentimental type, but inside he is. His favorite book is *Old Yeller.*

Quieting down after a show, Donnie sometimes feels lonely even though he's got four of the greatest friends a guy ever had right there. He knows someday there will be a very special girl in his life. But Donnie hasn't met her yet.

Once he thought he had, but it wasn't right. She dropped him twice. That really hurt, but they're friends now, and Donnie's more careful about getting involved. Still, he loves to be in love!

Maybe he's just not ready. But Donnie knows his special girl is out there somewhere. If the dream of becoming a rock star can come true…anything can happen! Peace out.

SECOND STOP:
A Week With
Jon in London

Jon Knight loves to travel. If you believe in astrology, it's all in the stars. Jon's a Sagittarian, born on November 29. Sagittarians live for maps, suitcases, and foreign phrases.

Jon's lucky. The New Kids travel more than any other band in the world—probably a hundred times as far as the average person travels in a lifetime!

One of the things Jon likes about travel is the way it keeps a person open-minded. He loves trying new things, and he's open to all kinds of movies, TV shows, and music (except heavy metal).

Before joining the New Kids, none of the guys had traveled very much. Donnie had never even been outside Boston! Now they've played all over the world, even down under in Australia.

Jon likes London. It's a bit like him—hip but traditional; polite and proper but full of fashion and fun. He also relates to the British passion for dogs and horses.

Jon slips on a rugby shirt, jeans, and a pair of sunglasses for a private walk with his Shar-pei puppy, Nikko. He likes to give Nikko lots of personal care and attention. On the road, Jon keeps the puppy's food in Tupperware containers and gives him Evian water to drink. But more than mineral water, Nikko loves a good walk.

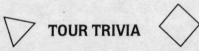 **TOUR TRIVIA**

5. Backstage, Jon pays special attention to fans from the Make-a-Wish Foundation, a group that...

    a. grants the wishes of seriously ill children
    b. gives to charities
    c. holds annual picnics
    d. buys stock in candle factories

They enter St. James's Park near Downing Street, where the prime minister lives. It's great to have a quiet time with Nikko, who barks at the geese and a gangly pelican. England reminds Jon of summers at his grandparents' cottage in Canada.

Sometimes he misses quiet times like this, but being with the New Kids is definitely worth the sacrifice. The band members have been called the five hardest-working kids in show business, but Jon doesn't mind. As long as the work's there, Jon will gladly do it. He wants the band to go as far as it can!

Jon thinks it makes life more exciting if you try to be the best at everything you do. And if the guys keep working this hard, they can keep traveling. There are still quite a few faraway spots Jon wants to see!

Sometimes Jon worries that success will change him and his friends in the band. But he figures if it hasn't happened yet, it's not going to.

He sees clouds reflected in the shimmering lake. A loon lands gracefully, sending rings of ripples into the water to meet the ripples made by its mate. All this beauty—the only thing that's missing is the right girl to share it with.

Jon's dream girl is someone pretty much like himself. He thinks "alikes" attract, not opposites.

Whoever Jon's dream girl is, she'll have to be independent, because this busy New Kid isn't always around. He appreciates a girl who can take care of herself and who has her own successful career. Jon wants someone sweet and smart, who's easy to talk to, and fun to be with. It wouldn't matter what they did on a date, as long as they were together.

That's the problem with Tiffany. Jon really likes the sweet pop singer, and they have so much in common. But it's nearly impossible to get together now that they're on separate tours. Still, there's always the telephone and memories. Jon and Tiffany had a great time at her eighteenth birthday party. Mel's Diner, at Universal Studio's Streets of the World, is a really funky spot.

Jon knows that someday he'll find that special girl and the time to be with her. But right now he's been spotted by fans!

Gentlemanly Jon takes time out for autographs. He tries never to disappoint New Kids fans.

It's hard to explain to them that sometimes the guys are busy or not in the mood. Some fans even get rude if they don't get to meet their favorite New Kid. Jon tries to smooth things over, but when fans don't understand, it sometimes gets frustrating.

He reminds himself that greeting fans is part of his everyday work—to them it's often a once-in-a-lifetime event. So he tries to make it special. Jon asks fans questions about themselves, what their favorite songs are, where they're from.

It's fun when things can be spontaneous. Jon remembers one time when the group was driving along in the limo and they spotted some girls in New Kids T-shirts. The New Kids rolled down the window and chatted with the fans like friends.

Sometimes having fans is embarrassing, like the time Jon was in a hotel Jacuzzi and suddenly realized that all these fans were staring at him. He felt like a fish in an aquarium!

Jon usually laughs when fans do crazy things. But sometimes it feels like fans want a piece of him, which is kind of scary.

Of course, British girls are polite. Jon wishes he could stay and talk with them longer, but as Danny would say, "I'm outta here!"

When there's a moment free from work, Jon loves to sneak out for a bit of incognito shopping. If he wears sunglasses and a hat, Jon can usually get around pretty well without being recognized—at least for a while.

He's dying to hit the stores of London, which have always been a great place to shop. The town was originally called Londinium, and was a trading post way back in A.D. 43—at least, that's what the guidebook says.

The best way to get to the stores is on one of London's famous red double-decker buses. Jon's hoping to get a bunch of gifts for the folks back in Boston—and, of course, some new clothes. They don't call him GQ for nothing!

Harrods is a giant department store on Brompton Road in the ritzy Knightsbridge section of London. Jon has no trouble finding things he likes at Harrods. Conservative British style is right up his alley. Jon likes clothes that are neat but casual, with just a touch of funk.

Harrods also has plenty of Jon's favorite striped rugby shirts, and there's no trouble finding his size— large. He hunts down some dark-colored socks and baggy shorts, available in his favorite colors, basic black and white.

When you travel with people, you really get to know them well. Lately, Jon finds he can walk through a store and know just the things Donnie, Danny, and Joe would like. And Jordan's always been easy to shop for—he loves to borrow Jon's clothes. Too bad he's always leaving junk in the pockets! Jon gets his revenge by dumping the pockets out on Jordan's bed. That's brothers for you!

Jon decides that if he ever needs a business suit, he'll come back to London. The Savile Row tailors are famous for being perfectionists. Many people in London still have their clothes hand-fitted instead of buying them "off the peg." For now, Jon's happy with good old American jeans!

It's time to get ready for the day's press confer- ence and photo session. As big brother to all the guys (not just Jordan), Jon tries to keep things running smoothly. Peter Work, the New Kids' road manager, and Jon keep things on schedule.

Jon is organized and hates messes! He often winds up picking up after the other guys. When you're as busy as the New Kids, it's hard to stay neat. Jon reminds the guys to get their laundry done. The wardrobe people take care of a lot of the group's clothes, but the guys wash their own personal stuff, like jeans. They're used to doing their own wash at home, and there's no sense getting spoiled on the road.

Jordan complains that Jon is always telling the guys to be good and mind their manners. When there are many people looking up to you, manners are important. Besides, look how far the Brits have gotten by being polite!

Lots of times Jon helps the guys pick out their outfits for shoots or TV tapings. They didn't like wearing matching sequins when they first started out. The Fab Five think it's important for each New Kid to express his own personality with his clothes. But they also like to look good together onstage. It's a question of balance, being supportive of each guy's individuality in the team.

Dana, the group's stylist, pulls a dazzling array of pants, shirts, vests, and jackets from the giant wardrobe trunks. But who's going to wear what? Jon sees a shirt he doesn't like, and Dana laughs when she catches Jon hiding it in the couch cushions.

Donnie is so outrageous! Jon never knows if he's going to show up with his jeans on inside out, or what. Right now Donnie's clowning around in his bathrobe, waiting for Uncle Rob, the special wardrobe assistant, to finish a hem.

Jon loves Danny's sense of drama. Today he's got

on one of his wild print shirts with a paisley vest. Leather jackets give Danny that street look. Both guys like spending lots of time putting outfits together and shopping in urban boutiques.

 TOUR TRIVIA

6. Crazed fans have...
   a. popped out of hotel garbage cans
   b. stretched out on the ground in front of the New Kids' limo
    c. disguised themselves as maids to surprise the New Kids in their hotel rooms
   d. all of the above

Joe wants to know how he looks. Cute as ever, of course, in his crownless hat, leather jacket, and jeans. Jon thinks Joe is the most "normal" dresser in the group. He thinks it's neat that Joe still looks like a kid.

Since Jon's the first one ready, he buys the other guys some time by going out to talk to the press. Sometimes all five guys talk to them together; at other times, just one New Kid or a few will take care of the many interviews.

Jon thinks the funniest part is reading about themselves afterward. Sometimes the reporters get confused about which New Kid is which. He hates it when a really ugly picture of himself is printed, but the boys often get to choose the pictures used for their posters and pinups.

Jon once felt shy about giving interviews, but he's used to it now. He loves the reporters' British accents.

The photo shoot is at Buckingham Palace—just in time for the changing of the guard. It's easy to remember this is a royal city; everywhere you look there are crowns, even on the telephone booths, lamp-posts, and door knockers.

This giant old brick mansion is still the home of the royal family. Donnie wonders if Charles and Di are home!

Earth to Danny! Jon smiles to get Danny's atten-tion and to remind him to pay attention to the pho-tographer. Sometimes Danny goes off into his own world, thinking. But Donnie never forgets the camera. He's mugging a mile a minute!

Everyone stares when the Queen's cavalry rides up. They make sure the Queen stays protected during the changing of the guard.

The mounted soldiers look like they just rode off the pages of a picture book. Their horses are beautiful, and so well groomed! The guards wear the most splendid uniforms: gold helmets with flame-red plumes, red and gold epaulets on their shoulders, and gleaming breastplates and swords. Their jackets are black with red piping, and the guards also wear starched white gloves, white trousers, and high, glossy black boots.

Jon wonders what it would be like to climb into those clothes every morning. In fact, seeing them on their horses makes him wonder what it would be like to be a real "knight."

Jon wishes there was time to go riding again. He's not an experienced rider yet, but hopes to do more. Maybe he'll get to try out the bridle path in Hyde Park.

Jon also likes swimming and skiing, and wouldn't mind trying cricket, which is the sport in England that is closest to baseball. He thinks it would be funny if The Crickets played cricket!

The cavalry rides away, and the sun seems to go with them. It looks like some of London's famous bad weather is on the way.

The photographer quickly snaps a whole roll of film—some shots of each Kid alone, some of the whole group. Jon hopes he looks handsome and wonders if he should have worn his new shirt.

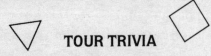

TOUR TRIVIA

7. The Fab Five first met Tiffany

    a. at a party
    b. in her dressing room
    c. at one of their concerts
    d. on the Arsenio Hall show

28

No use worrying now—the shoot's over. The Kids rush inside before it really starts to pour.

Jon glimpses a street musician taking shelter in a doorway, an old man clutching his accordion. A chalk artist stands up to watch the first drops drown his masterpiece, but he doesn't seem to mind at all.

Jon guesses Londoners are used to rain. It's a good excuse to duck inside for "a spot of tea." Jon would be just as happy with a strawberry shake and Hostess cupcakes, but this world traveler can also enjoy a real English tea with scones heaped with strawberry jam and clotted cream. Cheerio!

THIRD STOP:
On the Bus
With Jordan
in New York City

Jordan reads mail in the back of the bus and opens a gift from a fan: a soap-on-a-rope microphone! He starts singing into it, of course.

Then Jordan decides to play reporter.

"If you could eat only one food for the rest of your life, what would it be?" he asks Jon, sticking the "microphone" in his brother's face. Jordan would pick lasagna and chocolate milk shakes, and wonders if Jon would, too.

"Lasagna," Jon says. "No, maybe..."

"Me want cookie," Donnie interrupts, doing the *Sesame Street* Cookie Monster.

Joe tosses a box of Oreos to Donnie.

"I can't wait to eat some good Mexican food," Joe adds, staring out the window for a few seconds before returning his attention to the schoolbooks in his lap.

The New Kids are on their way to New York City, rolling down a highway in their home away from home, the bus. The Kids spend more than half their time traveling between gigs, busing it whenever they're going less than five hundred miles.

Three buses carry the backup band, bodyguards, equipment, and crew. It usually takes ten to twelve hours to get from one concert to the next.

Fortunately, the Fab Five have everything they need right on the bus: a living room with a sofa, stereo, TV and VCR, video games, a refrigerator, bathroom, and bunk beds.

Jordan is used to bunks. When he was little, he shared the top bunk with Jon, while their older brothers, David and Chris, shared the bottom. At least now they each have their own bed—even if it is moving at fifty-five miles per hour.

The guys sleep as much as they can on the bus. The bunks are pretty comfortable. But with their nonstop schedule, they're lucky to get six hours sleep a night while on tour.

The New Kids watch TV shows and movies, and have some pretty lively discussions about which ones are best. All agree on *Cheers* and *America's Most Wanted*. As far as movies go, some of the guys' favorites are: *Big, Tootsie, Fright Night, Rambo*, and lots more. They're all into Brian De Palma movies. Jordan's favorite movie is *The Untouchables*, but

A quick fan photo before the New Kids hit the stage.

Joe makes eye contact with a special fan.

Sexy Jon likes to travel and try new things.

Jordan drives the crowd wild.

Danny sings to fortunate fans in the front row.

Donnie sings the hit song "Hangin' Tough."

The New Kids on the Block leave fans screaming for more.

Joe and Donnie cruising with the top down.

Donnie likes *Scarface* better.

The Fab Five actually met film director Brian De Palma at a post-concert party in New York. They talked about movies, of course. The Kids thought De Palma was way cool!

They also love cartoons and have a library of five hundred cartoon tapes, including plenty of Danny's favorite, Woody Woodpecker. The Kids sometimes call Danny Woody. All the guys are into video games, so it was really great when Nintendo gave them some game sets and a bunch of awesome accessories.

Naturally, the Kids spend a lot of time on the bus listening to music. Jordan's taste really depends on his mood. The Stylistics have been Jordan's favorite group since he was a little kid. The Fab Five love rhythm and blues, rap, and most rock, but no heavy metal!

Jordan thinks being on the bus is like being on the longest family car trip ever, only you're traveling with your best friends. The secret to getting along is having as much fun as possible on the way!

The Kids have been together so long that the whole tour company feels like a big, happy family. They love their bodyguards, Robo, Tony, Al, and Bisquit, aka "the Big B." Bisquit looks incredibly tough, but he's really a teddy bear.

Most of the time, their road manager, Peter Work, is working—just like his name! But when he's not, Peter likes to joke around, and they all have a really good time.

Living in close quarters gets hectic. Sometimes the guys fight, but they never stay mad for long. And a lot of their arguments end in food fights, laughter, or wrestling. Deep down, all the Kids like each other and know it, so why worry about the little things that grate on nerves?

Everyone has a few bad habits. Jordan can't stop biting his nails or twirling his hair! And sometimes he really puts his foot in his mouth. But nobody's perfect. The good news is that the New Kids are all easygoing.

Now that the Fab Five are maturing, they don't bicker as often. In fact, they seem to get closer every day. Jordan thinks the key to getting along is knowing when to give one another time alone. They're all individuals, not just New Kids on the Block.

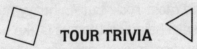

TOUR TRIVIA

8. At the 1989 Macy's Thanksgiving Day parade in New York City, the New Kids sang...

    a. "I'll Be Loving You (Forever)"
    b. "This One's for the Children"
    c. "Jingle Bells"
    d. the national anthem

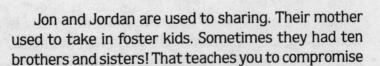

Jon and Jordan are used to sharing. Their mother used to take in foster kids. Sometimes they had ten brothers and sisters! That teaches you to compromise and to respect others' privacy.

The guys are friends because they're really friends, not just because of the group. Some groups have separate buses for each member, but the New Kids enjoy hanging out together. If New Kids ended tomorrow, they'd still be tight. They even spend time together when they're not on tour. The Kids really care about each other.

Lots of times, the Fab Five just sit around and talk. Even though they've been friends for a long time, it seems like they never run out of things to say. The five of them can talk about anything.

Discussions range from serious to silly. One minute they're talking about problems like homelessness and pollution, the next minute they're all agreeing that Hot Wheels were their favorite childhood toys.

Once the New Kids smoke-bombed the crew's tour bus—but only once, because the crew got mad! The crew knows to watch out if the guys get their hands on a can of Silly String. New Kids love that stuff!

When the call for chow comes, it's nothing fancy. The Kids miss home cooking, but they're usually more hungry than picky. Jordan loves to put catsup on everything, especially Northside burgers. Being famous has not changed what the guys like to eat— Mickey D's and Oreo cookies.

Now that the New Kids are away so much, they all really appreciate their families. The experience of being in the New Kids has brought them closer to their loved ones. The guys try to meet their families on the road as much as they can.

When Jon gets homesick, he cuddles his puppy, Nikko. Sometimes Jordan reads fan mail, which reminds him of the many people who care about the New Kids. There's always plenty of fan mail on hand, especially during prom season and on the boys' birthdays. Jordan's favorite fan letters are the funny ones. And last year he sent out two hundred valentines!

The Fab Five all do their share of autographing albums, pictures, and giveaways from local radio stations and national teen magazines.

Jordan's favorite way to spend time on and off the bus is making music. That's why the Kids always have musical equipment on hand.

Sometimes the bus is a great place to come up with a new song. Jordan loves it when he starts singing and playing and everybody joins in.

The Kids usually pull into a new city during the early morning hours. The crew gets there even earlier to set up the stage. The guys either stay asleep on the bus or check into a hotel for a few more hours sack time.

Jordan doesn't usually get up early in the morning, but he's glad he opens his eyes in time to catch a glimpse of dawn on the New York skyline. Orange light twinkles off hundreds of windows and sparkles on the Hudson River.

After sleep, the Fab Five take the limo downtown from the hotel to their rehearsal. They travel through the theater district on Broadway. They see giant billboards for movies and musicals, and a million tourist shops spilling out onto the sidewalks crowded with people of every shape, race, and size. Pigeons rise in a great swooping cloud past the bronze statue in Herald Square.

Donnie and Joe drop to their knees and sing, "Give My Regards to Broadway" so loud that the sides of the bus rattle, and it almost drowns out the din of traffic outside.

Jon reads a street sign and exclaims, "Fashion Avenue!"

"Stop the bus for GQ!" Jordan teases.

Jon can't wait to get out and shop, and neither can the rest of the Kids. New York has the funkiest boutiques! But first—rehearsal.

Some people would get tired of playing music day after day, but Jordan loves it! His favorite childhood memory is singing in a church choir. And nothing beats the feeling of singing onstage.

Rehearsals are fun, too, because the Kids have a chance to play with the music and try new things. Maurice Starr, the group's producer, has written hundreds of songs, and the New Kids are all now working on writing, too, so there's plenty of material to choose from.

The Fab Five have been working really hard on their music—and getting better all the time! They practice during sound checks every day, and at home between tours.

Jon's getting really good on bass. Joe's gotten a good start on learning guitar.

Inspired by Jordan's skill, Danny is working hard at the piano. Jordan's favorite musician, Maurice, is teaching him keyboards. Jordan also admires Prince and Teddy Riley.

TOUR TRIVIA

9. The New Kids consider the highlight of their career...

   a. hearing their first hit song on the radio
   b. winning best pop/rock album and best group at the American Music Awards
   c. receiving a standing ovation at the Apollo Theater in Harlem
   d. having three albums simultaneously on *Billboard's* hit chart

The younger Knight has always loved music. He comes from a musical family. Jordan's grandparents knew how to read music. His father plays piano, his mother plays accordion, and brother David plays bass guitar.

All aspects of music interest Jordan. Along with Danny and Donnie, he's hoping to become a record producer. The Crickets (the boys' writing/production/engineering team) are getting better all the time. They produced several songs on the new album.

Jordan aspires to be a songwriter and maybe even a solo artist. But first he wants to stay with the New Kids for a long time. Why stop when you're having so much fun?

Jordan loves working with other musicians. There's so much you can learn from one another—and it's fun to jam.

Donnie and Jordan wrote a song called "Turn on the Radio" with Tommy Paige. They also do the backup vocals, along with Danny and Michael Jonzun (Maurice Starr's brother).

"T" (Tommy) and Jordan got to be good friends when Tommy opened for the New Kids on tour. The two musicians got stuck in a hotel lobby because they weren't allowed to leave the hotel without security. There was a piano in the lobby, and Tommy started to play.

T had been opening for the Fab Five for a while already, but with his suit and tie and serious manner, none of the New Kids had really gotten to know him. But Jordan couldn't help looking over T's shoulder that day.

Tommy was playing this really great song. And it

turned out to be one he'd written himself! T and Jordan started talking, then T moved over on the bench so Jordan could play one of his songs. It was "I'll Be Your Everything."

T got really excited. He said, "I've got goose bumps on my arms. It must be a hit song!"

By the end of that tour, all the New Kids were great friends with Paigey. Later, they recorded "I'll Be Your Everything" with T, and it really helped his career!

The New Kids still find it hard to believe all their fame and good fortune. Jordan used to listen to the radio and think, "I wish that could be me." And now it's a dream-come-true.

Rehearsal's over. The New Kids have one whole hour to hit the shops. But first Jordan's going to get a haircut at Astor Place Hair Stylists, which is a funky old barbershop where all the punks get their hair spiked.

On the way, the Kids read the signs above the stores that crowd one another along the busy avenue. Hippie print dresses hang like butterflies in one window under the sign TAJ MAHAL IMPORTS.

This is the wholesale district, where clothes, jewelry, and all kinds of goods come into the city and then are sold to the department stores and boutiques where regular people shop.

There's a store just for belts and watchbands, another for party favors and paper plates, and one that's only for bridal veils.

"It's the Flatiron Building!" Danny gasps.

The Fab Five turn to look at a building that juts into the intersection of Broadway and Twenty-third Street and Fifth Avenue like the prow of a ship breaking an ocean of traffic. The Flatiron Building is shaped like a tower of triangles, its old stones gritty with exhaust fumes.

Everywhere the guys look there seems to be graffiti. Some of the artists are really talented, but it isn't a good thing to do. Jordan used to be a graffiti pest, but music is a much better way to express yourself than writing on walls. Music's more fun, and you don't get in trouble!

They arrive at Astor Place. Jordan loves watching the people here. You see everything! There's a punk girl in black leather, her pink hair in spikes all around her head, and she's arm in arm with this little old lady who's got to be her grandmother. In Greenwich Village, everyone is as outrageous as Donnie.

Astor Place Hair Stylists looks like an old barbershop you might find in a train station, except for the pictures of patrons on the wall. People who think Jordan's hairstyle is funky ought to get a look at these! It's hard to believe human hair can do that, and how do people with those haircuts ever sleep?

Jordan just wants his usual side part, stripe 'n' tail. He looks in the mirror and smiles. He's still self-conscious about the clear braces he got last

41

November. But when they come off, Jordan will have perfect teeth.

Having earrings in both ears is a souvenir from the Kids' trip to London. Guys in that country get both ears pierced.

 TOUR TRIVIA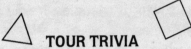

10. **Who's opened for the New Kids?**
    a. **Sweet Sensation**
    b. **Dino**
    c. **Tiffany**
    d. **all of the above**

Reflected in the mirror, Jordan can see a mob of fans gathering outside. Between snips, Reynaldo, the barber, says people often stop to watch the hair fall at Astor Place. But never this many!

Outside the New Kids sign autographs, then jump back into the limo to ride down to Tower Records. You can get just about any kind of music there.

Someday Jordan would like to have his own apartment in the Big Apple. Until then, it's back to the bus!

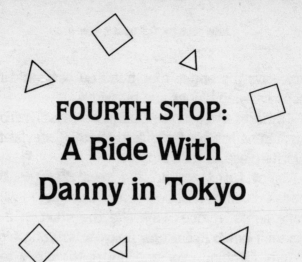

FOURTH STOP:
A Ride With
Danny in Tokyo

Tokyo is one of the most amazing places Danny Wood has ever seen—and as a member of New Kids on the Block, he's seen a lot of places! Huge towers of steel and glass soar above a maze of streets teeming with people all moving at an incredible pace. If New York's funk, then Tokyo's rap.

The group rides a freeway to the taping of a Japanese commercial for Sony CD players. Japanese people are really into New Kids on the Block! The Kids are also going to be on a popular Japanese TV show called *Funky Tomato.*

Before Danny joined the New Kids, he was planning to become an architect. It really excites him to see the different designs of buildings in the countries the New Kids visit.

Tokyo looks like a city of the future, but the guidebook says it's about four hundred years old. Tokyo keeps growing bigger and better.

"E ticket attraction!" Donnie shrieks. The E ticket attractions are his favorite rides at Disneyland—his favorite place to take a date!

Danny turns around and sees that the limo is headed uphill on a ribbon of highway dotted with red brake lights. It does look like the start of a roller coaster ride! But it's only Tokyo's amazing highway system, climbing over and under the city's tangled web of neighborhoods.

When the limo pulls up to the TV station, the New Kids are greeted by a crowd of cheering but orderly fans. Danny thinks it's really great that the group has fans all over the world. He believes that if everyone can dance together, then maybe they can live in peace!

He tries to stay focused during the taping, but it's hard not to be distracted by all the super high-tech equipment—Danny wants to know how every knob works! The more he learns about sound recording, the more he wants to learn.

When he was eighteen, Danny gave up a four-year scholarship to Boston University to give his all to the New Kids. When he goes back, Danny will probably major in electrical engineering and become a recording engineer. No, not just *a* recording engineer—he wants to be the best!

Jordan and Donnie feel the same way. That's why

they formed a writing, engineering, and production company with Danny called The Crickets.

Danny really likes the name. The guys wanted it to sound like a gang—but a good gang. There's one rap group called Jamaican Dog Posse, and they thought, "Let's be the Mice Posse." What's more harmless than a mouse? Then they came up with The Crickets, because crickets make music.

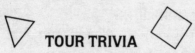

▽ TOUR TRIVIA ◇

11. **Who does the New Kids' "mikes and stuff" on tour?**
    a. **Peter Work**
    b. **Rodney Fisher**
    c. **Joe Montana**
    d. **Danny Wood**

The New Kids know what it's like growing up on the streets. All of them are from pretty rough neighborhoods. They didn't have fields to play ball in, so they played on the streets.

That's where Danny learned how to break dance. But if you aren't careful, it's easy to get into trouble on the streets.

The New Kids were lucky. Maurice Starr, their producer, gave them a chance to be something special. Danny hopes to reach other street kids through the group's music. He wishes he could say to all the fans, "Stay off the streets and hold on to your dreams."

Danny tries to see as much as he can of what the technicians are doing during the shoot. It's exciting. Every year, the machines are getting more advanced. By using computers with digital recording equipment, music and recording people can produce and change any sound in the world! And with advances in computer programming...

"Danny! Earth to Woody, come in Woody." Jon teases Danny out of his trance because the shoot is over. Sometimes he really gets lost in his own world!

The New Kids say good-bye to the photographer, sound technicians, crew, and Sony executives. There's a lot of bowing, because that's what people do in Japan. It's kind of fun.

People are very courteous in Japan, maybe because this small island is so crowded. If people weren't polite, things would get really hairy. It's kind of like the five New Kids being together all the time on the bus. Each guy has to be considerate of the others to keep everybody happy.

Joe rolls down the limo window, and in blows a whiff of something that smells good! The guys are hungry after the shoot, but not sure what the food stand is selling.

Nobody can decide what to eat. The restaurant windows are filled with plates of plastic food. It's easier than reading a Japanese menu, and some of it looks really funny—like the plastic strands of spaghetti holding up a fork.

Many places have American food as well as Japanese. Danny wants to try sushi, raw fish and rice wrapped in seaweed, but the guys vote for Mickey D's.

Yes, there is a McDonald's in Tokyo! It's pretty much like a McDonald's at home, only here they serve bean sprouts on the burgers instead of lettuce. And if you want, you can try a tofu burger. Jon and Jordan are just happy to have their favorite shakes.

After they eat, the New Kids shop for souvenirs. Whenever they are on tour, the New Kids try to buy presents for their families back home. The guys stop at a shop filled with beautiful painted kites made from bamboo and paper. There are so many cool kites that Danny doesn't know which one to get for his mother. But he finally decides on one painted with a Japanese mask. It's really neat, and it's in his favorite colors, red and black.

Carved wooden hair combs are also traditional Japanese keepsakes. The guys stop at another shop, where a man carves a comb out of special fragrant wood. Joe buys one for his sister, Carol.

In another store, Donnie buys a handmade doll for his younger sister, Rachel.

Back in the limo, Danny rolls down the window to get a better look at a woman wearing traditional

Japanese clothes. Her bright silk kimono and painted umbrella are beautiful. They seem out of place in this modern city. But that's Tokyo!

The limo passes a pachinko parlor, which is like an arcade. Pachinko is a popular Japanese pinball game. Donnie wants to stop—all the New Kids love games—but there just isn't time.

The New Kids also like Sumo Wrestling, which is a little like pro wrestling. Sumo wrestlers are cool, but Danny thinks samurai and ninjas are even cooler. He wonders if he can get a ninja outfit. It'd be great to work out in, and maybe even to wear onstage.

 TOUR TRIVIA

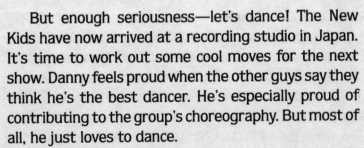

12. **The New Kids have not yet toured...**
    a. **England**
    b. **Japan**
    c. **Australia**
    d. **Tibet**

But enough seriousness—let's dance! The New Kids have now arrived at a recording studio in Japan. It's time to work out some cool moves for the next show. Danny feels proud when the other guys say they think he's the best dancer. He's especially proud of contributing to the group's choreography. But most of all, he just loves to dance.

When he's a recording engineer, he plans to do

everything he can to help new groups get started, the way Maurice helped the New Kids. Donnie's already doing that with a rap group.

Danny would also like to write songs, and keep on singing and dancing, of course. And he's determined to keep at the piano lessons. He's hoping someday he'll play as well as Jordan.

Meanwhile, he's gaining experience. Whenever the New Kids stay more than two nights in a hotel, Dick Scott, their manager, arranges for recording equipment to be sent to their rooms. Or, if they're playing in a big city, they go to a recording studio.

Recording on the road gives the New Kids a jump on their next album. The vocals are recorded on tour. Instrumental tracks are recorded in Boston by top studio players. But someday the New Kids will play their own instrumentals, too!

By the time the guys leave the recording studio, it's dusk. Fortunately, they've missed the rush hour. Tokyo's in such a rush all the time, Danny would hate to see that!

Lights switch on along the glittering Ginza strip— a long street of bars and restaurants. But Danny just wants a piece of fruit and a nice warm bed.

The limo joins the stream of traffic on one of the many freeways. Jordan admires the long, blurring lines of red and white lights, and he wonders if he can work that into a song.

Danny wishes there were time to see a Kabuki play—they're supposed to be amazing. All the parts are played by guys—kind of like the New Kids' Christmas show! Unfortunately, performances last anywhere from five to six hours. The only time the guys have that much leisure is on the bus!

Danny would like some time alone. That's something that's really hard to find on tour—and so important to this thoughtful loner.

Before New Kids, Danny used to spend a lot of private time keeping a diary or just thinking. Now he snatches moments to remove himself from all the craziness and just be good ol' Danny Wood, that guy from Boston.

The other guys understand, and they give Danny some space back at the hotel. Sometimes he's a chatterbox, the life of the party. And at other times Danny just needs to be alone.

Everybody seems to think he's such a tough guy, but inside, sometimes, he's insecure. He'll get down on himself for being too short and square-headed. It makes Danny blush when fans act like he's handsome. Danny doesn't think he's anywhere near as handsome as Jordan. But he's the best he can be!

There's one woman who understands complex Danny—his mom. When he's on tour, sometimes it's just great to pour out his feelings in a letter to her.

Mom knows all his strengths and weaknesses—like being determined and disciplined but also stubborn and defensive. She knows he's not really a trouble-maker at heart; he's just a bit wild.

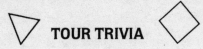 **TOUR TRIVIA**

13. What do the New Kids find wherever they go?

    a. fans
    b. McDonald's
    c. more fans
    d. all of the above

Danny asks his mom to say hi to everybody—Dad, Melissa, Beth, Pam, Brett, and Rachel. When he writes to her, it feels like he's home, in the big Boston house jammed with love.

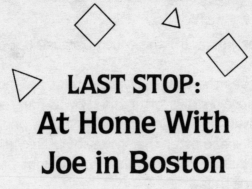

LAST STOP:
At Home With
Joe in Boston

Joe naps backstage at the Worcester Centrum. He's facedown on the couch, still wearing sneakers. His teddy bear's fallen on the floor.

Jon jostles Joe's shoulder. It's time to get up for the show. It takes Joe a minute to remember where he is. He picks up his teddy bear and remembers: The Kids are in Boston. They're home!

After all the weeks of homesickness, it's hard to believe they're finally here. Sometimes on the road, Joe tells himself not even to think of home. He puts everything aside and just works. But if he feels really homesick, he hugs his teddy bear and pretends he's at home, hanging out with his brothers and sisters or sleeping in his very own bed.

But the Kids are home now. It's Joe's birthday (December 31, New Year's Eve)—and there's a show to do! Joe jumps off the couch because it's time to get ready.

Joe loves the way everyone buzzes around backstage before a show. After the show is fun, too.

The New Kids always like to meet and greet fans before and after the shows, but today it's even more special. Lots of people have brought presents for Joe's birthday.

There are flowers and cards and even more gifts than usual. Joe is touched to realize fans know what he likes—teddy bears, hugs, and Oreo cookies. He can't stop smiling. Everyone's being so nice!

Joe's so happy to see his family. It's like he can't hug them enough, it's so great to see them all again.

His oldest sister, Judy, is up from New York. Alice is here from Vermont. His parents are here with Susan, Patricia, Carol, Jean, Kate, and Tom.

It's Carol's birthday, too, so there's going to be a big family celebration after the show. Joe can't wait to give Carol the comb he bought for her in Japan!

Joe's so used to the guys calling him Joe, Joey, or Bird that it's funny to hear his mother call him Joseph. It seems like everywhere he turns, there's love. It's great!

Joe thinks it's cool to be the youngest, even if he does get teased a lot. With the teasing comes a lot of love and attention. Besides, he's used to being the youngest at home.

The hardest thing for Joe was gaining the acceptance of the group. The other guys all went to school together, and he was from a different neighborhood. Also, Joe was replacing a friend of theirs who was leaving the group. For a while, they resented him, even though it wasn't his fault.

 TOUR TRIVIA

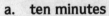

14. At the Boston Against Drugs benefit performance, fans went so wild the New Kids had to stop playing after only...

    a. ten minutes
    b. three songs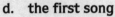
    c. one minute
    d. the first song

P.S. Backstage, the boys wrote a check for $25,000 to the antidrug organization.

Besides all that, Joe was only twelve when he joined the New Kids. The other guys were older. It took the guys a while to become friends, but now they're as close as brothers.

Because he was so young when he joined, Joe grew up in the group. He had to learn to sing a whole new way when his voice changed. Today he's turning seventeen—time flies when you're having fun!

Some people think the New Kids happened overnight. But the boys spent a lot of time working up to success. Joe always wanted to be in show business.

Actually, the first thing he wanted to be was a bricklayer (his dad is vice president of the Boston Bricklayers Union). But it turned out that show business was in Joe's blood.

As soon as he could walk, Joe was dancing. One of the kiddie pictures his mother sent to a fan magazine shows a little boy with a top hat and cane, singing his heart out. It's strange for Joe to look at that little kid and realize that boy is him. But he remembers the feeling, the joy of singing and dancing—because he still feels it every time he's onstage.

When he was six, Joe sang in a big group of children that was part of the Neighborhood Children's Theatre of Boston. His family was supportive. They're very accepting of one another, which has helped give Joe the confidence to perform.

Everybody in the McIntyre family loves show business. Joe's sister Judy starred on *The Guiding Light, One Life to Live, Ryan's Hope,* and two episodes of *Spenser: For Hire.* She's always auditioning—who knows what she'll play next!

Joe's mother has always been an actress in community theater. Seeing her in shows was a big event in Joe's childhood. The whole McIntyre clan has performed together in community stage shows— except Joe's dad, who was cheering in the audience.

All the McIntyres love to sing and dance, but Kate's the best dancer. Carol's an actress and has performed with the Boston Children's Theatre. Susan sings. Tricia's in school plays. Alice is a teacher, which is really a lot like performing. And even though Tommy doesn't perform, he's very talented.

Judy and Joe have performed together a couple of times. When he was really little, Joe and Judy were in a nonprofessional production of the musical *Oliver!* Joe loved it!

They also played in *Our Town* together. Joe played Judy's brother—that was easy. The hard part was the third act. It takes place in a cemetery, and Joe played a dead person sitting in a chair. He couldn't move at all for the whole act. That was rough!

Joe heard about the New Kids audition when he was still singing with the Neighborhood Children's Theatre of Boston. He met Maurice Starr on Father's Day in 1985. He sang one of the songs the New Kids were going to record for their demo tape.

Afterward, he was riding in a car with Mary Alford, the talent manager who helped Maurice develop the New Kids. Mary said, "Well, do you want to be in the group? You've got the part."

Amazing! And, of course, Joe said yes.

It took a while for the New Kids to take off. For one thing, they weren't called the New Kids in the beginning. Maurice liked the name NYNUK for some reason.

The Kids didn't like it because it was too weird, and their friends teased them about it.

 TOUR TRIVIA

15. **April 24 is New Kids on the Block Day in...**
    a. **Australia**
    b. **Dorchester**
    c. **Massachusetts**
    d. **Minnesota**

The name changed when the group recorded Maurice's song "New Kids on the Block." The guys felt like the lyrics were their own life stories. Maurice agreed that the new name expressed more of what the group was really about.

The New Kids played small theaters and clubs for about five years, getting used to performing together and waiting for their big break. All the guys felt they'd make it, but it didn't happen overnight.

In fact, they were all pretty disappointed when their first album didn't do well. That was followed by more disappointments. First "Be My Girl" came out, and it went only to number ninety on the charts. Then "Stop It Girl" came out and didn't do anything. "Didn't He Blow Your Mind" did all right, but it didn't go into the Top Ten until it came out as the flip side to "Cover Girl" last year. For a while, nothing clicked.

But Joe wasn't worried, because he had a feeling something was going to happen. He knew the New Kids' time would come. They just needed a chance—which turned out to be opening for Tiffany.

The red-haired pop star gave the boys a chance to open for her, even though at the time the New Kids were a no-name band. Tiffany's popularity opened a new door. Her fans became New Kids fans—once they heard the band's music!

For a while, the Kids led pretty much normal lives, performing only one night every few weeks. They felt a little like Cinderella—at night at the ball they were pop stars, then the next day they went back to being ordinary schoolkids.

These days Joe still leads that sort of double life—no wonder he's always taking naps! Along with all the work of being in the group, he still has a year and a half to go in school.

Last semester, Joe made the honor roll, but it wasn't easy! He has to get up early every morning while the band's on the road, and study with a traveling tutor.

If he misses school time for a press conference or whatever, Joe has to make it up the next day. Lots of times, while the other guys get to practice their instruments or learn about recording, Joe has homework to do.

It's kind of tough missing out on regular high

school. The other guys already had most of their high school years, but Joe was just getting into high school when the group started touring.

On a typical touring day, Joe starts school around eight A.M. He'll eat breakfast, then the guys will go to a mall or something. Then they perform for the sound check, practice, and play around on their instruments. Joe plays a little keyboard, and he's learning guitar.

The guys usually go back to the hotel to relax and get something to eat. They shower around six, then return to the venue and get ready for the show.

Whatever happens after a show is up in the air, but the New Kids never go out to clubs. A lot of the time they just go back to their rooms for some much-needed sleep.

Sometimes Joe knows he should rest, but he hates missing out on the fun! He likes when there's time to make friends with a fan and she'll show the guys around her city.

Joe doesn't mind living out of a suitcase. He's become quite a skilled packer. He can fit fifteen shirts and a dozen pairs of jeans, plus underwear and socks, into one standard suitcase.

Joe's life isn't all work and school. He likes football, bicycle riding, bowling, skiing, golf, and video games. And sometimes he just likes being silly!

In the meet-and-greet room, fans come rushing up to Joe. He reads about himself in the teen magazines, but it's still hard to believe all these girls have crushes on him.

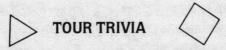 **TOUR TRIVIA**

16. The New Kids were greeted by over three thousand screaming fans at...

    a. their high school in Boston
    b. New York's Rockefeller Center
    c. the Hawaii airport
    d. their first concert

Joe tries to be nice to everyone. When a girl has trouble with her flash, he fiddles with her camera until it works. She's thrilled. Joe loves making someone's day!

His ideal girl is charming, friendly, and caring—cool, smart, and nice, with a fabulous sense of humor. Joe's idea of a great date is a trip to Disney World. With all the rides and exhibits, you can't miss having a good time!

The guys get in a huddle when it's almost time to go on. Joe hears the fans screaming, "We want the New Kids!" The group runs out onstage.

Joe's ears fill with screams. The crowd is up! Adrenaline pumps.

Tonight's a special show. Donnie gets the whole

audience singing "Happy Birthday" to Joe. He can't believe it. It's so great!

After the show, there's a party at the hotel, but Joe can't wait to get to the family party at home. The whole McIntyre clan's gathered. There's singing and dancing and joking around.

The McIntyres always get silly at parties. They do things like picking up tennis racquets and pretending they're guitars, singing show tunes at the top of their lungs, or imitating TV sportscasters.

When the cake comes out, Joe counts the candles. He's seventeen! He'll be getting his driver's license this year, and maybe even a car!

Joe thinks the 3.25 BMW is the ultimate, but he probably won't get such a fancy car. He's not sure what color he wants, red, white, or blue, but definitely wants a cellular phone.

Everybody says, "Make a wish," so Joe tries to think of something.

He wishes there were an end to homelessness.

Joe blows out the candles, and there's a lot of cheering and hugging and well-wishing. Everyone hopes the New Kids will continue to be successful.

There's lots to look forward to in the year ahead: a New Kids Saturday morning cartoon show, movie and publishing deals, and who knows what else?

Joe is determined to be a musical success, but his most important personal goal is to have peace of mind. He's concerned with the problems in the world, like war, poverty, and drugs. And he hopes the New Kids can continue to help charities like United Cerebral Palsy. Joe believes we all have to chip in to make this a better world.

Some people think we're headed for destruction. But Joe thinks the future can be great if we make it happen. People can either destroy the world or make it almost perfect. If the New Kids fans grow up to be smart, we'll have a nice clean world.

All Joe's relatives want to know if he plans on going to college. He won't until New Kids has a rest period, because he wants to take a full course load, to take it seriously, and not work while he's in school. Joe wants to major in journalism or communications. English is his favorite subject.

But right now, all he wants to think about is being home! Boston is his favorite vacation spot, and home is his all-time favorite place to be.

Joe even likes doing chores around the house, like cutting grass and fixing the fence. He likes things at home to be perfect, and why pay someone to do what you can have fun doing yourself?

Joe also likes hanging out, watching *Monday Night Football*, and, of course, sleeping in his own bed. There's nothing like it. Good night, teddy!

TOUR TRIVIA
Answers

1.	d	9.	c
2.	b	10.	d
3.	a	11.	b
4.	d	12.	d
5.	a	13.	d
6.	d	14.	c
7.	b	15.	c
8.	b	16.	c